In memory of my GninGnin, Fung Tai Look
—L. L.

For my Marraine, Nancy Smoller Le Floch
—S. T. J.

I would like to thank the Washington Crab Producers in West Port, Washington,
and the crab shakers who work there, especially Rosalvai, Diane, Betty and Debbie.

Please note that there is no standard transliteration for Taishanese. All Chinese phrases in
this story are the author's own application of romanization to the patois spoken by nearly all
Chinese immigrants from the 1800s through the 1960s.
—L. L.

Atheneum Books for Young Readers
An imprint of Simon & Schuster
Children's Publishing Division
1230 Avenue of the Americas, New York, New York 10020
Text copyright © 1999 by Lenore Look
Illustrations copyright © 1999 by Stephen T. Johnson
All rights reserved including the right of reproduction in
whole or in part in any form.
The text of this book is set in Eva Antiqua.
The illustrations are rendered in pastel and
watercolor on Ingres paper.
First Edition
Printed in Hong Kong
10 9 8 7 6 5 4 3 2

Library of Congress Cataloging-in-Publication Data.
Look, Lenore.
Love as strong as ginger / by Lenore Look ;
illustrated by Stephen T. Johnson.—1st. ed.
"An Anne Schwartz book."
Summary: A Chinese American girl comes to
realize how hard her grandmother works to fulfill
her dreams when they spend a day together at the
grandmother's job cracking crabs.
ISBN 0-689-81248-5
1. Chinese Americans—Juvenile fiction. [1. Chinese Americans—
Fiction. 2. Grandmothers—Fiction.
3. Work—Fiction.] I. Johnson, Stephen T., date., ill. II. Title.
PZ7.L8682Gr 1999 [E]—dc20 96-43459

GLOSSARY

Chiubungbung (CHEW bung bung): Stinky-stinky. Since Chinese words repeat for emphasis, this means a *very* bad smell.

Chong: A cannery or factory.

Chowing: Frying food quickly in a little fat.

Doong: A sticky rice cake wrapped in bamboo leaves, often filled with pork, salted duck yolk, peanuts, or red-bean paste.

GninGnin (NYIN NYIN): Paternal grandmother. Literally translated means "person-person," or the fullness of two people.

Taishanese: A southern dialect from the western Pearl River delta region of China.

AUTHOR'S NOTE

This story was inspired by my grandmother, who worked in a Seattle cannery in the 1960s and 70s. She was among the older immigrant women, mostly from Southeast Asia, who, because they lacked English and job skills, did the only work they could find: shaking crab. The work paid very little: three pennies for every pound of crabmeat. On a good day, working rapid-fire, my grandmother might have earned six dollars, tops. Though Seattle canneries are gone now, and my grandmother has passed away, it isn't hard for me to remember that time in our lives when I lived without yesterday or tomorrow and Grandma served heaven on a spoon.

A pair of large rubber gloves that smelled of the sea used to hang in my grandma's kitchen.

"GninGnin, may I try those on?" I asked one day.

"Chiubungbung," she replied, meaning stinky-stinky in Taishanese, our Chinese dialect. She broke noodles into a pot of boiling water, and shoved the gloves away from us. Steam rose into her face.

I spent nearly every Saturday with GninGnin in her Chinatown apartment while Mother and Father went to work. She taught me how to make *doong*, sticky rice dumplings wrapped in bamboo leaves, and I taught her how to dress a Barbie doll. At lunchtime, she'd make the best meal, clearing room for me in her tiny kitchen where salted butterfish and flounder hung like laundry above our heads.

"I wear my gloves for cracking crabs at the crab *chong*," she explained as she peeled shrimp, my favorite, into the pot, "to keep the jagged shells from cutting my hands." As she reached for some chives to cut into our soup, I looked at her hands. Her skin was baggy around the fingers, and delicate, like the rice paper around candy. Her gloves were the opposite: thick, with patches from a tire repair kit.

"Why do you crack crab?" I asked.

"Only job I could find," she said. "Nobody wants to hire an old woman who can't speak English." She tasted the soup on her dark wooden spoon, then ladled some into bowls. The chives floated like confetti among the shrimp.

"Maybe if I knew English," she said, "I would have become . . . a famous actress!"

"Really?" I stared at my grandma. She posed her head like the movie stars on the calendars the shopkeepers gave her at Christmas. Her eyes twinkled.

"Sure," she said. "Katie, in America, you can become whatever you dream."

"I want to be like you," I said, following her into the next room.

She set our bowls on a table and we sat down on smooth, old stools. "Will you take me to the crab chong?" I asked.

"You want to go there?" She chuckled. "Little dream."

"How do you crack crab?"

"With a mallet." She made a pounding fist. "Then I shake out the meat. They pay me for every pound that I shake out. I can do two hundred pounds a day, enough for bus fare and a fish for dinner . . . and someday, maybe enough to help you go to college."

I slurped my soup. "Is crab tasty?" I asked.

GninGnin picked the shrimp from her bowl and put them in mine. "I don't eat crab. Tastes like hard work."

"Maybe if I'm there, your work will go faster," I said. "I'll crack a hundred crabs for you!"

GninGnin's eyes grew big. "One hundred crabs!" she exclaimed. "This I've got to see."

It was cold the morning my grandma took me to the crab chong. Rain misted our faces and the sky was pebble-dark as we waited, hand in hand, for the bus. When it came, it was crowded with ladies clucking their tongues in singsong languages. They looked like friends on an outing, each sporting rubber gloves, a rubber apron, and tall rubber boots. The bus was chiubungbung. I wrinkled my nose and played a game of holding my breath.

"Where are your gloves?" an old lady in a quilted jacket asked me in our Taishanese.

"No size fits her," GninGnin replied.

"May that always be so," the lady nodded, smiling a gold tooth.

When the bus stopped, I followed GninGnin to a tall building overlooking dark waters. My sneakers turned wet and cold as we passed a man hosing shell and creamy crab guts into the spaces between the planks.

Inside, chiubungbung billowed out from large, hot vats. GninGnin stretched a nylon net over my hair and tied on a bandana to keep me from getting a "crabhead"—a headful of crabmeat. "It's the rules," she whispered. "No one is allowed to look pretty here." Everyone tied on their aprons, and stuffed sponges into the palms of their gloves.

Suddenly, a bell rang and we hurried into a warm room filled with a zillion crabs! The orange hard-shell formed a mountain range that seemed to go on forever. Steam rose from the crabs and covered everything.

GninGnin disappeared into the fog. Then a terrible deafening noise began. Mallets swung fast and faster. Hands flew, tossing shell and keeping meat. I covered my ears.

I found GninGnin standing behind a crab mountain, moving quickly, forcefully, unlike the way she moved in her kitchen. **Crack!** The tip of a claw came off. GninGnin's whole body shook as she banged her hand on the rim of a small metal box to shake out a few hairs of meat. Then she grabbed another claw. **Crack!** The upper part of the claw split open. **Bang!** Out came a chunk of meat.

Her face grew pink. Crabmeat strands stuck to her cheeks. I moved away. "Don't talk to anyone," she yelled after me. "Every minute is another penny!"

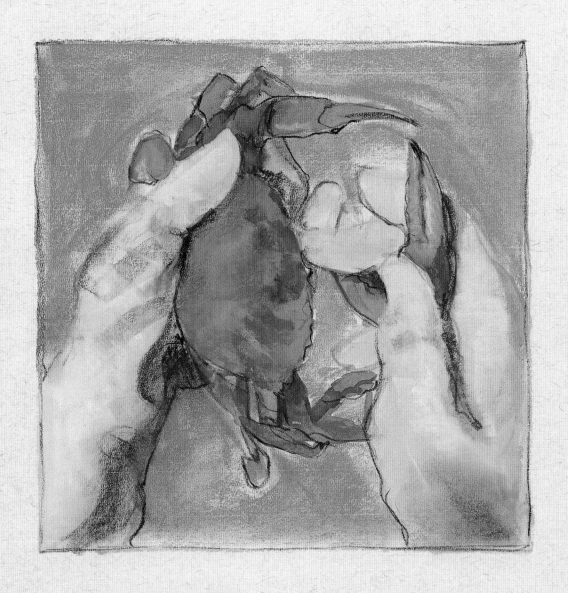

In a corner, one of GninGnin's friends was giving the crabmeat a bath. When she stirred in a shovelful of salt, meat floated and shell pieces sank. She scooped a handful of the meat onto a conveyor belt that moved it under a purple light where others picked out more shell.

The crabmeat fell into another bath before going to a lady with cans. "Restaurants and stores can't get enough of our crab," said the can lady, popping a small piece into my mouth. It melted like butter. "Good for crab cakes, crab imperial, crabmeat stuffing, crab soup, everything."

I watched until my feet hurt and my stomach growled. Then I wandered back, crunching over empty claws. I found GninGnin standing in the same spot, but now she was covered with tiny, cream-colored hairs. She looked like a strange bird.

"I need to sit down," I moaned.

"There's only one place to sit—on the toilet upstairs," Gnin Gnin replied. She continued to work, but her arms looked heavy; she moved slowly.

The sun had traveled across the windows above her head and the crab chong had grown quiet again.

"How do you keep going?" I asked.

"I don't know . . ." she began.

Then she stopped and lifted her head, blinking away crabmeat. Her face brightened.

"Don't you know that I'm a famous actress making a movie in a crab chong? All around us is the movie set and the other actors. How can I give up when I'm the star?"

Finally, GninGnin reached for the last crab. She turned and held out her mallet. "Would you like to do this one?"

"Yes," I said, eagerly snatching the warm handle. GninGnin tied her apron around me. I put my hands in her roomy gloves and stepped into her place.

With all my strength I hammered at the back of the crab. But nothing happened. I hit it again. Nothing. "It's a bad crab," I complained.

GninGnin laughed. I laughed. Her friends gathered and everyone laughed at my bad crab.

A man with cheeks as orange as cooked crab shell and boots as tall as trees stomped over through the broken shells. "Who have we here?" he boomed. "Are you my newest employee?"

"She's just here to watch her grandma," a lady replied in English for GninGnin.

The man stared at GninGnin. She stared at the crab in front of me. I stared at the gloves hanging on my hands.

"Would you like a job, young lady?" he asked.

I shrugged. "The gloves don't fit."

"How about taking that crab for dinner then?" he said, offering it to me.

I looked at GninGnin. She nodded. "Thanks," I said.

On the ride home, I sat close to GninGnin. Her work done, she was sitting with her eyes closed, her head rocking with the bus. Tears leaked out of the corners of her eyes; she was tired. Her gloves rested on her knees.

That afternoon, GninGnin soaked me in a hot bath to wash the chiubungbung from my hair and skin. Then she prepared my crab.

"You were right, Katie," she said, *chowing* scallions, ginger, and black-bean paste with the crab. "You made my work easier."

"But I forgot to help," I said. "And I'm not strong enough to crack crab!"

She gave me a taste of something delicious on her spoon. "You're strong enough to do other things . . . to become whatever you dream."

I ate GninGnin's words and the wonderful meal she'd
prepared for me. Crab chong special, she called it. "Made with
love as strong as ginger and dreams as thick as black-bean paste."
And I filled myself with all the flavors of her hard work.